The Course of True Love (and First Dates)

A MAGNUS BANE STORY

By Cassandra Clare

First published in Great Britain 2014 by Walker Books Ltd
87 Vauxhall Walk, London SE11 5HJ

This edition published 2018

2 4 6 8 10 9 7 5 3 1

Text © 2014 Cassandra Claire LLC
Previously published in *The Bane Chronicles* and as an individual eBook
Cover illustration © 2018 Dan Funderburgh

The right of Cassandra Clare to be identified as author of this
work has been asserted by her in accordance with the
Copyright, Designs and Patents Act 1988

This book has been typeset in Dolly

Printed and bound by CPI Group (UK) Ltd, Croydon CR0 4YY

British Library Cataloguing in Publication Data:
a catalogue record for this book is available from the British Library

ISBN 978-1-4063-7961-7

www.walker.co.uk

This is for the people—they know who they are—
who write letters and e-mails, and come up at signings,
and say Magnus and Alec mean a lot to them.

Like Magnus, you are magical and you are heroes.

Alec's eyes were a little wide. Magnus suspected that he had been acting on reflex and had not actually intended to use force meant for demon foes against a mundane.

The redheaded guy squawked, revealing braces, and flapped his hands in what seemed to be either urgent surrender or a very good panicked duck impression.

It was Friday night in Brooklyn, and the city lights were reflecting off the sky: orange-tinted clouds pressing summer heat against the sidewalks like a flower between the pages of a book. Magnus walked the floor of his loft apartment alone and wondered, with what amounted to only mild interest, if he was about to be stood up.

Being asked out by a Shadowhunter had been among the top ten strangest and most unexpected things that had ever happened to Magnus, and Magnus had always endeavored to live a very unexpected life.

He had surprised himself by agreeing.

This past Tuesday had been a dull day at home with

the cat and an inventory list that included horned toads. Then Alec Lightwood, eldest son of the Shadowhunters who ran the New York Institute, had turned up on Magnus's doorstep, thanked him for saving his life, and asked him out while turning fifteen shades between puce and mauve. In response Magnus had promptly lost his mind, kissed him, and made a date for Friday.

The whole thing had been extremely odd. For one thing, Alec had come and said thank you to Magnus for saving his life. Very few Shadowhunters would have thought of doing such a thing. They thought of magic as their right, due whenever they needed it, and regarded warlocks as either conveniences or nuisances. Most of the Nephilim would as soon have thought of thanking an elevator for arriving at the right floor.

Then there was the fact that no Shadowhunter had ever asked Magnus out on a date before. They had wanted favors of several kinds, magical and sexual and strange. None of them had wanted to spend time with him, go out to a movie, and share popcorn. He wasn't even sure Shadowhunters *watched* movies.

It was such a simple thing, such a straightforward request—as if no Shadowhunter had ever broken a plate because Magnus had touched it, or spat "warlock" as if it were a curse. As if all old wounds could be healed, made as though they had never been, and the world could become the way it looked through Alec Lightwood's clear blue eyes.

At the time, Magnus had said yes because he wanted to say yes. It was quite possible, however, that he had said yes because he was an idiot.

After all, Magnus had to keep reminding himself, Alec wasn't even all that into Magnus. He was simply responding to the only male attention he'd ever had.

Alec was closeted, shy, obviously insecure, and obviously hung up on his blond friend Trace Wayland. Magnus was fairly certain that was the name, but Wayland had reminded Magnus inexplicably of Will Herondale, and Magnus didn't want to think about Will. He knew the best way to spare himself heartbreak was not to think about lost friends and not to get mixed up with Shadowhunters again.

He had told himself that this date would be a bit of excitement, an isolated incident in a life that had become a little too routine, and nothing more.

He tried not to think of the way he'd given Alec an out, and how Alec had looked at him and said with devastating simplicity, *I like you.* Magnus had always thought of himself as someone who could wrap words around people, trip them up or pull the wool over their eyes when he had to. It was amazing how Alec could just cut through it all. It was more amazing that he didn't even seem to be trying.

As soon as Alec had left, Magnus had called Catarina, sworn her to secrecy, and then told her all about it.

"Did you agree to go out with him because you think the Lightwoods are jerks and you want to show them you can corrupt their baby boy?" asked Catarina.

Magnus balanced his feet on Chairman Meow. "I do think the Lightwoods are jerks," he admitted. "And that does sound like something I'd do. *Damn* it."

"No, it doesn't really," said Catarina. "You're sarcastic twelve hours a day, but you're almost never spiteful. You have a good heart under all the glitter."

Catarina was the one with the good heart. Magnus knew exactly whose son he was, and where he came from.

"Even if it was spite, no one could blame you, not after the Circle, after all that happened."

Magnus looked out the window. There was a Polish restaurant across the street from his house, its flashing lights advertising twenty-four-hour borscht and coffee (hopefully not mixed together). He thought of the way Alec's hands had trembled when he'd asked Magnus if he wanted to go out, about how glad and astounded he had seemed when Magnus said yes.

"No," he said. "It's probably a bad idea—it's probably my worst idea this decade—but it had nothing to do with his parents at all. I said yes because of him."

Catarina was quiet for a few moments. If Ragnor was around he would have laughed, but Ragnor had disappeared to a spa in Switzerland for a series of complicated facials meant to bring out the green in his complexion. Catarina had the instinct of a healer: she knew when to be kind.

"Good luck on your date, then," she said at last.

"Much appreciated, but I don't need good luck; I need assistance," said Magnus. "Just because I'm going on this date does not mean it will go well. I'm very charming, but it does take two to tango."

"Magnus, remember what happened the last time you tried to tango. Your shoe flew off and nearly killed someone."

"It was a metaphor. He's a Shadowhunter, he's a Lightwood, and he's into blonds. He's a dating hazard. I need an escape strategy. If the date is a complete disaster, I'll text you. I'll say 'Blue Squirrel, this is Hot Fox. Mission to be aborted with extreme prejudice.' Then you call me and you tell me that there is a terrible emergency that requires my expert warlock assistance."

"This seems unnecessarily complicated. It's your phone, Magnus; there's no need for code names."

"Fine. I'll just text 'Abort.'" Magnus reached out and

drew his fingers from Chairman Meow's head to his tail; Chairman Meow stretched and purred his enthusiastic approval of Magnus's taste in men. "Will you help me?"

Catarina dragged in a long, annoyed breath. "I will help you," she promised. "But you've called in all your dating favors for this century, and you owe me."

"It's a bargain," said Magnus.

"And if it all works out," said Catarina, cackling, "I want to be best woman at your wedding."

"I'm hanging up now," Magnus informed her.

He had made a bargain with Catarina. He had done more than that: he had called and made reservations at a restaurant. He had selected a date outfit of red Ferragamo pants, matching shoes, and a black silk waistcoat that Magnus wore without a shirt because it did amazing things for his arms and shoulders. And it had all been for nothing.

Alec was half an hour late. The probability was that Alec's nerve had broken—that he had weighed his life, complete with his precious Shadowhunter duty, against a date with a guy he didn't even like that much—and he was not coming at all.

Magnus shrugged philosophically, and with a casualness he did not quite feel, padded over to his drinks cabinet and made himself an exciting concoction with unicorn tears, energizing potion, cranberry juice, and a twist of lime. He'd look back on this and laugh one day. Probably tomorrow. Well, maybe the day after. Tomorrow he'd be hungover.

He might have jumped when the buzzer sounded through the loft, but there was nobody but Chairman Meow there to see. Magnus was perfectly composed by the time Alec ran up the stairs and hurtled through the door.

Alec could not have been described as perfectly composed. His black hair was going in every direction, like an octopus that had been dropped in soot; his chest was rising and falling hard under his pale-blue T-shirt; and there was a light sheen of perspiration on his face. It took a lot to make Shadowhunters sweat. Magnus wondered exactly how fast he had been running.

"Well, this is unexpected," said Magnus, raising his eyebrows. Still holding his cat, he had flung himself lightly on the sofa, his legs hooked over one of the carved wooden arms. Chairman Meow was draped over his stomach and meowing in perplexity about the sudden change in his situation.

Magnus might have been trying a bit too hard to appear louche and unconcerned, but judging by Alec's crestfallen expression, he was really pulling it off.

"I'm sorry I'm late," Alec panted. "Jace wanted to do some weapons training, and I didn't know how to get away—I mean, I couldn't tell him—"

"Oh, Jace, that's it," said Magnus.

"What?" said Alec.

"I briefly forgot the blond one's name," Magnus explained, with a dismissive flick of his fingers.

Alec looked staggered. "Oh. I'm—I'm Alec."

Magnus's hand paused mid-dismissive-flick. The gleam of city lights through the window reflected off the blue jewels on his fingers, casting bright blue sparks that caught fire and then tumbled and drowned in the deep blue of Alec's eyes.

Alec had made an effort, Magnus thought, though it took a trained eye to spot it. The light-blue shirt fit him considerably better than the unholy gray sweatshirt that Alec had been wearing on Tuesday. He smelled vaguely of cologne. Magnus felt unexpectedly touched.

"Yes," said Magnus slowly, and then he smiled slowly as well. "Your name I remember."

Alec smiled. Maybe it didn't matter if Alec did have a little thing for Apparently-Jace. Apparently-Jace *was* beautiful, but he was the sort of person that knew it, and they were often more trouble than they were worth. If Jace was gold, catching the light and the attention, Alec was silver: so used to everyone else looking at Jace that that was where he looked too, so used to living in Jace's shadow that he didn't expect to be seen. Maybe it was enough to be the first person to tell Alec that he was worth being seen ahead of anyone in a room, and of being looked at longest.

And silver, though few people knew it, was a rarer metal than gold.

"Don't worry about it," said Magnus, swinging himself easily off the couch and pushing Chairman Meow gently onto the sofa cushions, to the Chairman's plaintively voiced dismay. "Have a drink."

He pushed his own drink hospitably into Alec's hand; he hadn't even taken a sip, and he could make himself a new one. Alec looked startled. He was obviously far more nervous than Magnus had thought, because he fumbled and then dropped the glass, spilling crimson liquid all over himself and the floor. There was a crash as the glass hit the wood and splintered.

Alec looked like he had been shot and was extremely embarrassed about it.

"Wow," said Magnus. "Your people are really overselling your elite Nephilim reflexes."

"Oh, by the Angel. I am so—I am so sorry."

Magnus shook his head and gestured, leaving a trail of blue sparks in the air, and the puddle of crimson liquid and broken glass vanished.

"Don't be sorry," he said. "I'm a warlock. There's no mess I can't clean up. Why do you think I throw so many parties? Let me tell you, I wouldn't do it if I had to scrub toilets myself. Have you ever seen a vampire throw up? Nasty."

"I don't really, uh, know any vampires socially."

Alec's eyes were wide and horrified, as if he was picturing debauched vampires throwing up the blood of the innocent. Magnus was prepared to bet he didn't know any Downworlders socially. The Children of the Angel kept to their own kind.

Magnus wondered what exactly Alec was doing here in Magnus's apartment. He bet Alec was wondering the same thing.

It might be a long night, but at least they could both be well-dressed. The T-shirt might show Alec was trying, but Magnus could do a lot better.

"I'll get you a new shirt," Magnus volunteered, and made his way to his bedroom while Alec was still faintly protesting.

Magnus's closet took up half his bedroom. He kept meaning to enlarge it. There were a lot of clothes in it that Magnus thought would look excellent on Alec, but as he riffled through them, he realized that Alec might not appreciate Magnus imposing his unique fashion sense on him.

He decided to go for a more sober selection and chose the black T-shirt that he had been wearing Tuesday. That was perhaps a little sentimental of Magnus.

The shirt admittedly had BLINK IF YOU WANT ME written on it in sequins, but that was about as sober as Magnus got. He tugged the shirt off its hanger and waltzed back into the main room to find that Alec had already taken his own shirt off and was standing around somewhat helplessly, his stained shirt clenched in his fist.

Magnus stopped dead.

The room was illuminated only by a reading lamp; all the other light came from outside the windows. Alec was painted with streetlights and moonlight, shadows curling around his biceps and the slender indentations of his collarbones, his torso all smooth, sleek, bare skin until the dark line of his jeans. There were runes on the flat planes of his stomach and the silvery scars of old Marks snaked around his ribs, with one on the ridge of his hip. His head was bowed, his hair black as ink, his luminously pale skin white as paper. He looked like a piece of art, chiaroscuro, beautifully and wonderfully made.

Magnus had heard the story of how the Nephilim were created many times. They had all left out the bit that said: *And the Angel descended from on high and gave his chosen ones fantastic abs.*

Alec looked up at Magnus, and his lips parted as if he was going to speak. He watched Magnus with wide eyes, wondering at being watched.

Magnus exercised heroic self-control, smiled, and offered the shirt.

"I'm—sorry about being a lousy date," Alec muttered.

"What are you talking about?" Magnus asked. "You're a fantastic date. You've only been here ten minutes, and I already got half of your clothes off."

Alec looked equal parts embarrassed and pleased. He'd told Magnus he was new to all this, so anything more than mild flirting might scare him off. Magnus had a very calm and normal date planned: no surprises, nothing unexpected.

"Come on," said Magnus, and grabbed a red leather duster. "We're going to dinner."

*

The first part of Magnus's plan, getting the subway, had seemed so simple. So foolproof.

It had not occurred to him that a Shadowhunter boy was not used to being visible and having to interact with the mundanes.

The subway was crowded on a Friday night, which was not surprising but did seem to be alarming to Alec. He was peering around at the mundanes as if he had found himself in a jungle surrounded by menacing monkeys, and he was still looking traumatized by Magnus's shirt.

"Can't I use a glamour rune?" he asked, as they boarded the F train.

"No. I'm not looking like I'm alone on a Friday night just because you don't want mundanes staring at you."

They were able to grab two seats, but it didn't appreciably improve the situation. They sat awkwardly side by side, other people's chatter rushing all around them. Alec was utterly silent. Magnus was fairly sure he wanted nothing more than to go home.

There were purple and blue posters staring down at them, showing elderly couples looking sadly at one another. The posters bore the words WITH THE PASSING YEARS COMES ... IMPOTENCE! Magnus found himself staring at the posters with a sort of absent horror. He looked at Alec and found that Alec could not tear his eyes away either. He wondered if Alec was aware that Magnus was three hundred years old and whether Alec was considering exactly how impotent one might become after that much time.

Two guys came onto the train at the next stop and cleared a space right in front of Magnus and Alec.

One of them began to dance by swinging himself dramatically around the pole. The other sat cross-legged and started beating time on a drum he'd carried in with him.

"Hello, ladies and gentlemen and whatever else you got!" the dude with the drum called out. "We're gonna perform now for your entertainment. I hope you'll enjoy it. We call it ... the Butt Song."

Together they began to rap. It was quite obviously a song they had written themselves.

"Roses are red, and they say love's not made to last,
But I know I'll never get enough of that sweet, sweet ass.
All that jelly in your jeans, all that junk in your trunk,
I just gotta have it—one look and I was sunk.
If you ever wonder why I had to make you mine,
It's 'cause no other lady has a tush so fine.
They say you're not a looker, but I don't mind.

What I'm looking at is the view from behind.
Never been romantic, don't know what love means,
But I know I dig the way you're wearing those jeans.
Hate to see you leave but love to watch you go.
Turn back, then leave again—baby do it slow.
I'm coming right after, gonna make a pass,
Can't get enough of that sweet, sweet ass."

Most of the commuters seemed stunned. Magnus was not sure if Alec was just stunned or if he was also deeply scandalized and privately commending his soul to God. He was wearing an extremely peculiar expression on his face and his lips were very tightly shut.

Under normal circumstances Magnus would have laughed and laughed and given the buskers a lot of money. As it was, he was profoundly grateful when they reached their stop. He did fish out a few dollars for the singers as he and Alec left the train.

Magnus was reminded again of the extreme disadvantages to mundane visibility when a skinny freckled guy slipped by them. Magnus was just thinking that he might have felt a hand snaking into his pocket when the guy gave a combination howl and screech.

While Magnus had idly wondered if he was being pickpocketed, Alec had reacted like a trained Shadowhunter: he grabbed the guy's arm and threw him up in the air. The thief flew, outstretched arms limply wagging, like a cotton-stuffed doll. He landed with a crack on the platform, with Alec's boot on his throat. Another train rattled by, all lights and noise; the Friday night commuters ignored it, forming a knot of bodies in tight shiny clothes and artful hair around Magnus and Alec.

Alec's eyes were a little wide. Magnus suspected that he

had been acting on reflex and had not actually intended to use force meant for demon foes against a mundane.

The redheaded guy squawked, revealing braces, and flapped his hands in what seemed to be either urgent surrender or a very good panicked duck impression.

"Dude!" he said. "I'm sorry! Seriously! I didn't know you were a ninja!"

Alec removed his boot, and cast a hunted glance around at the fascinated stares of the bystanders.

"I'm not a ninja," he muttered.

A pretty girl with butterfly clips in her dreadlocks put her hand on his arm. "You were amazing," she told him, her voice fluting. "You have the reflexes of a striking snake. You should be a stuntman. Really, with your cheekbones, you should be an actor. A lot of people are looking for someone as pretty as you who'd do his own stunts."

Alec threw Magnus a terrified and beseeching look. Magnus took pity on him, putting a hand on the small of Alec's back and leaning against him. His attitude and the glance he shot at the girl clearly communicated *my date*.

"No offense," said the girl, rapidly removing her hand so she could dig in her bag. "Let me give you my card. I work in a talent agency. You could be a star."

"He's foreign," Magnus told the girl. "He doesn't have a social security number. You can't hire him."

The girl regarded Alec's bowed head wistfully. "That's a shame. He could be *huge*. Those eyes!"

"I realize he's a knockout," Magnus said. "But I am afraid I have to whisk him away. He is wanted by Interpol."

Alec shot him a strange look. "Interpol?"

Magnus shrugged.

"Knockout?" Alec said.

Magnus raised an eyebrow at him. "You had to know I

thought so. Why else would I agree to go on a date with you?"

Apparently Alec had not known for sure, even though he'd said Isabelle and Jace had both commented on it. Maybe the vampires had all gone home and gossiped about the fact Magnus thought one of the Shadowhunters was a dreamboat. Magnus possibly needed to learn subtlety, and Alec possibly was not allowed access to mirrors at the Institute. He looked startled and pleased.

"I thought maybe—you know you said you weren't unsympathetic—"

"I don't do charity," said Magnus. "In any area of my life."

"I'll give the wallet back," piped up a helpful voice.

The red-haired mugger interrupted what might have become a nice moment by scrambling to his feet, digging out Magnus's wallet, and then dropping

Magnus's wallet on the ground with a pained yelp.

"That wallet bit me!"

That'll show you not to steal warlocks' wallets, Magnus thought, bending down to retrieve the wallet from a forest of sparkling high heels on the concrete.

Aloud he said, "This just isn't your lucky night, is it?"

"Your wallet bites people?" Alec asked.

"This one bites people," said Magnus, pocketing it. He was glad to have it back, not only because he liked money but because the wallet matched his red crocodile-skin pants. "The John Varvatos wallet bursts into flames."

"Who?" said Alec.

Magnus gazed at Alec sadly.

"Totally cool designer," chipped in the girl with butterfly clips. "You know, they give you designer stuff free when you're a movie star."

"I can always flog a Varvatos wallet," agreed the

red-haired mugger. "Not that I'd steal and sell anything belonging to anyone on this platform. Specially not you guys." He shot Alec a look that bordered on hero worship. "I didn't know gay dudes could fight like that. Like, no offense. It was badass."

"You have been taught two important lessons about tolerance and honesty," Magnus informed him severely. "And you still have all your fingers after trying to mug me on a first date, so this was the best outcome you could expect."

There was a murmur of sympathy. Magnus stared around and saw Alec looking a little wild-eyed and everyone else looking concerned. Apparently the crowd they had gathered truly believed in their love.

"Aw, man, I'm really sorry," said the mugger. "I wouldn't want to mess up anybody's first date with a ninja."

"WE ARE LEAVING NOW," said Magnus, in his best

High Warlock voice. He was worried that Alexander was planning to fling himself into the path of an oncoming train.

"Have fun on your date, boys," said Butterfly Clips, stuffing her card into the pocket of Alec's jeans. Alec jumped like a startled hare. "Call me if you change your mind about wanting fame and fortune!"

"Sorry again!" said their former mugger, waving a cheerful good-bye.

They left the platform amid a chorus of well-wishers. Alec looked as if he wished only for the sweet release of death.

The restaurant was on East 13th and 3rd, near an American Apparel store and among a row of tired-looking redbrick buildings. It was an Ethiopian and Italian fusion restaurant run by Downworlders. It was on the shady, shabby side, so Shadowhunters did not frequent it. Magnus had strongly suspected that Alec would not want to risk any Nephilim seeing them together.

He'd also brought many mundane dates there, as a way of easing them into his world. The restaurant wanted mundane custom but in the main the clientele were Downworlders, so glamours were used but fairly minimal.

There was a large graffitied dinosaur obscuring the sign. Alec squinted at it, but he followed Magnus inside the restaurant readily enough.

The moment Magnus stepped into the restaurant, he realized he'd made a terrible mistake.

The second the door closed behind them a terrible silence fell around the big, low-lit room. There was a crash as one diner, an ifrit with flaming eyebrows, dove behind a table.

Magnus looked at Alec and realized what they saw:

even if he wasn't wearing gear, his arms bore runes, and his clothes showed signs that he was wearing weapons. *Nephilim.* Magnus might as well have walked into a Prohibition-era speakeasy flanked by police officers holding tommy guns.

God, dating sucked.

"Magnus Bane!" hissed Luigi, the owner, as he scurried over. "You brought a Shadowhunter here! Is this a raid? Magnus, I thought we were friends! You could at least have given me a heads-up!"

"We're here socially," said Magnus. He held his hands up, palms out. "I swear. Just to talk and eat."

Luigi shook his head. "For you, Magnus. But if he makes any moves toward my other customers..." He gestured at Alec.

"I won't," Alec said, and cleared his throat. "I'm ... off-duty."

"Shadowhunters are never off-duty," said Luigi darkly, and dragged them to a table in the remotest part of the restaurant, the corner near the swinging doors that led to the kitchen.

A werewolf waiter with a wooden expression that indicated either boredom or constipation wandered over.

"Hello, my name is Erik and I will be your server this eve— Oh my God, you're a Shadowhunter!"

Magnus closed his eyes for a pained moment. "We can leave," he told Alec. "This may have been a mistake."

But a stubborn light had come into Alec's blue eyes. Despite his porcelain looks, Magnus could see the steel underneath. "No, that's fine, this seems ... fine."

"You're making me feel very threatened," said Erik the waiter.

"He's not doing anything," Magnus snapped.

"It's not about what he's doing, it's about how he's

making me *feel*," sniffed Erik. He slammed down the menus as if they had personally offended him. "I get stress ulcers."

"The myth that ulcers are caused by stress was debunked years ago," said Magnus. "It's actually some kind of bacteria."

"Um, what are the specials?" Alec asked.

"I can't remember them while my emotions are under this kind of strain," said Erik. "A Shadowhunter killed my uncle."

"I've never killed anyone's uncle," said Alec.

"How would you know?" demanded Erik. "When you're about to kill someone, do you stop and ask them if they have nephews?"

"I kill *demons*," Alec said. "Demons don't have *nephews*."

Magnus knew this to be only technically true. He cleared his throat loudly. "Maybe I should just order for both of us, and we can share?"

"Sure," said Alec, throwing his menu down.

"Do you want a drink?" the waiter asked Alec pointedly, adding *sotto voce*, "Or do you want to stab someone? If you absolutely have to, maybe you could stab the guy in the corner wearing the red shirt. He tips terribly."

Alec opened and shut his mouth, then opened it again. "Is this a trick question?"

"Please go," said Magnus.

Alec was very quiet, even after Erik the annoying waiter was gone. Magnus was fairly sure he was having a horrifying time, and could not blame him. Several of the other customers had left, casting panicked glances over their shoulders as they paid hurriedly.

When the food arrived, Alec's eyes widened when he saw Magnus had ordered their *kitfo* raw. Luigi had put in an effort: there were also luscious *tibs*, *doro wat*, a spicy red onion stew dish, mashed lentils and collards, and all of it laid out atop the thick spongy Ethiopian bread known as *injera*. The Italian part of Luigi's heritage was represented by a heap of *penne*. Alec did make short work of the food, and seemed to know he was supposed to eat with his fingers without being told. He was a New Yorker, Magnus thought, even if he was a Shadowhunter too.

"This is the best Ethiopian I've ever had. Do you know a lot about food?" Alec asked. "I mean, obviously you do. Never mind. That was a dumb thing to say."

"No, it wasn't," Magnus said, frowning.

Alec reached for a bite of *penne arrabiata*. He immediately began to choke on it. Tears streamed from his eyes.

"Alexander!" said Magnus.

"I'm fine!" Alec gasped, looking horrified. He snatched at his piece of bread first and only realized that it was bread when he tried to dab his eyes with it. He dropped the bread hastily and grabbed his napkin up instead, hiding both streaming eyes and scarlet face.

"You are obviously not fine!" Magnus told him, and tried a very tiny bite of the *penne*. It burned like fire: Alec was still wheezing into his napkin. Magnus made a peremptory gesture for the waiter that might have included a few blue sparks snapping and crackling onto other people's tablecloths.

The people eating near them were edging their tables subtly away.

"This *penne* is much too *arrabiata*, and you did it on purpose," said Magnus when the surly werewolf waiter hove into view.

"Werewolf rights," Erik grumped. "Crush the vile oppressors."

"Nobody has ever won a revolution with pasta, Erik," said Magnus. "Now go get a fresh dish, or I'll tell Luigi on you."

"I—" Erik began defiantly. Magnus narrowed his cat's eyes. Erik met Magnus's gaze and decided not to be a waiter hero. "Of course. My apologies."

"What a pill," Magnus remarked loudly.

"Yeah," said Alec, tearing off a new strip of *injera*. "What have the Shadowhunters ever done to him?"

Magnus lifted an eyebrow. "Well, he did mention a dead uncle."

"Oh," said Alec. "Right."

He went back to gazing fixedly at the tablecloth.

"He's still a total pill, though," Magnus offered. Alec mumbled something that Magnus could not make out.

It was then that the door opened and a handsome human man with deep-set green eyes came in. His hands were in the pockets of his expensive suit, and he was surrounded by a group of gorgeous young faeries, male and female.

Magnus slunk down in his chair. Richard. Richard was a mortal who the faeries had adopted in the way they did sometimes, especially when the mortals were musical. He was also something else.

Magnus cleared his throat. "Quick warning. The guy who just walked in is an ex," he said. "Well. Barely an ex. It was very casual. And we parted very amicably."

At that moment, Richard caught sight of him. Richard's whole face spasmed; then he crossed the floor in two steps.

"You are scum!" Richard hissed, and then picked up Magnus's glass of wine and dashed it in his face. "Get out while you can," he continued to Alec. "Never trust a warlock. They'll enchant the years from your life and the love from your heart!"

"Years?" Magnus spluttered. "It was barely twenty minutes!"

"Time means different things to those who are of faerie," said Richard, the pretentious idiot. "You wasted the best twenty minutes of my life!"

Magnus grabbed hold of his napkin and began to clean off his face. He blinked through the red blurriness at Richard's retreating back and Alec's startled face.

"All right," he said. "It's possible I was mistaken about the amicable parting." He tried to smile suavely, which was difficult with wine in his hair. "Ah well. You know exes."

Alec studied the tablecloth. There was art in museums given less attention than this tablecloth.

"Not really," he said. "You're my first ever date."

This wasn't working. Magnus didn't know why he had thought it might work. He had to get out of this date and not hurt Alec Lightwood's pride too much. He wished he could feel satisfaction that he had a plan in place for this, but as he texted Catarina under the table what he felt was a sense of enveloping gloom.

Magnus sat there silently, waited for Catarina to call, and tried to work out a way to say, "No hard feelings. I like you more than any Shadowhunter I've met in more than a century, and I hope you find a nice Shadowhunter boy ... if there are any nice Shadowhunter boys besides you."

His phone rang while Magnus was still mentally composing, the sound harsh in the silence between them. Magnus hastily answered. His hands were not entirely steady, and he was afraid for a moment that he would drop the phone as Alec had dropped his glass, but he managed to answer it. Catarina's voice filtered down the line, clear and unexpectedly urgent. Catarina was clearly a method actor.

"Magnus, there's an—"

"An emergency, Catarina?" Magnus asked. "That's terrible! What's happened?"

"An actual emergency happened, Magnus!"

Magnus appreciated Catarina's commitment to her role but wished that she would not shout so loudly right into his ear.

"That's so awful, Catarina. I mean, I'm really busy, but I suppose if there are lives at stake I can't say n—"

"There are lives at stake, you blithering idiot!" Catarina yelled. "Bring the Shadowhunter!"

Magnus paused.

"Catarina, I don't think you fully understand the point of what you're meant to do here."

"Are you drunk already, Magnus?" Catarina asked. "Are you off debauching and getting one of the Nephilim— one of the Nephilim who is under twenty-one—*drunk*?"

"The only alcohol that has passed my lips is the wine

that was thrown in my face," said Magnus. "And I was totally blameless in that matter as well."

There was a pause. "Richard?" said Catarina.

"Richard," Magnus confirmed.

"Look, never mind him. Listen carefully, Magnus, because I am working, and one of my hands is covered in fluid, and I'm only going to say this once."

"Fluid," said Magnus. "What kind of fluid?"

Alec goggled at him.

"Only going to say this once, Magnus," Catarina repeated firmly. "There is a young werewolf in the Beauty Bar downtown. She went out on the night of a full moon because she wanted to prove to herself that she could still have a normal life. A vampire called this in and the vampires are not going to be of any help because the vampires never are. The werewolf is changing, she is in an unfamiliar and crowded place, and she will probably lose control and kill somebody. I cannot leave the hospital. Lucian Graymark has his phone off, and the word from his pack is that he is in a hospital with a loved one. You are not in a hospital: you are out on a stupid date. If you went to the restaurant you told me that you were going to, then you are the closest person I know who can help. Will you help, or will you continue to waste my time?"

"I'll waste your time another time, darling," said Magnus.

Catarina said, and he could hear the wry smile in her voice, "I bet."

She hung up. Catarina was often too busy to say goodbye. Magnus realized he did not have all that much time himself, but he did waste a moment looking at Alec.

Catarina had said to bring the Shadowhunter, but Catarina did not have a great deal to do with the Nephilim. Magnus did not want to see Alec cut off some poor girl's head for breaking the Law: he did not want someone else to suffer if he made a mistake in judgment, and he didn't want to find himself hating Alec as he had hated so many of the Nephilim.

He also did not want mundanes to be killed.

"I'm so sorry about this," he said. "It's an emergency."

"Um," Alec said, hunching his shoulders, "it's okay. I understand."

"There's an out-of-control werewolf in a bar near here."

"Oh," said Alec.

Something inside Magnus cracked. "I have to go and try to get her under control. Will you come and help me?"

"Oh, this is a real emergency?" Alec exclaimed, and brightened immeasurably. For a moment Magnus felt pleased that a maddened werewolf was ravaging downtown Manhattan, if it made Alec look like that. "I figured it was one of those things where you arranged to have a friend call you so that you could get out of a sucky date."

"Ha ha," said Magnus. "I didn't know people did that."

"Uh-huh." Alec was already standing up, shrugging his jacket on. "Let's go, Magnus."

Magnus felt a burst of fondness in his chest; it felt like a small explosion, pleasant and startling at the same time. He liked how Alexander said the things that other people thought and never said. He liked how Alec called him Magnus, and not "warlock." He liked how Alec's shoulders moved under his jacket. (Sometimes he was shallow.)

And he was cheered that Alec wanted to come. He'd assumed that Alec might be delighted for the pretext to exit an uncomfortable date, but perhaps he'd read the situation wrong.

Magnus threw money down on the table; when Alec

made a demurring noise, he grinned. "Please," he said. "You have no idea how much I overcharge Nephilim for my services. This is only fair. Let's go."

As they went out the door they heard the waiter yell "Werewolf rights!" at their backs.

The Beauty Bar was usually crowded at this time on a Friday night, but the people spilling out of the door were not doing it with the casual air of those who had meandered outside to smoke or hook up. They were lingering under the shining white sign that had BEAUTY written in spiky red letters and what seemed like a picture of a golden Medusa's head underneath. The whole crowd had the air of people who were desperate to escape, yet who hovered, pinned in place by a horrified fascination.

A girl clutched Magnus's sleeve and gazed up at him, her false lashes dusted with silver glitter.

"Don't go in," she whispered. "There's a monster in there."

I am a monster, Magnus thought. *And monsters are his specialty.*

He didn't say it. Instead he said, "I don't believe you," and walked in. He meant it, too: the Shadowhunters, even Alec, might believe Magnus was a monster, but Magnus didn't believe it himself. He'd taught himself not to believe it even though his mother, the man he'd called his father, and a thousand others had told him it was true.

Magnus would not believe the girl in there was a monster either, no matter what she might look like to mundanes and Nephilim. She had a soul, and that meant she could be saved.

It was dark in the bar, and contrary to Magnus's expectations, there were still people inside. On a normal night the Beauty Bar was a kitschy little place full of happy people getting manicures from the staff, perched in the chairs that looked like old-fashioned hairdresser's chairs with massive hairdryers set up on the chair backs, or dancing on the black-and-white tiled floor that suggested a chessboard.

Tonight nobody was dancing, and the chairs were abandoned. Magnus squinted at a stain on the chessboard floor and saw that the black and white tiles were smeared with bright red blood.

He glanced toward Alec to see if Alec had noticed this too and found him shifting from foot to foot, obviously nervous.

"You all right?"

"I always do this with Isabelle and Jace," said Alec. "And they're not here. And I can't call them."

"Why not?" Magnus asked.

Alec blushed just as Magnus realized what he meant. Alec couldn't call his friends because he didn't want them to know he was on a date with Magnus. He especially did not want Jace to know. It was not a particularly pleasant thing to think about, but it was Alec's business.

It was also true that Magnus certainly didn't want any more Shadowhunters in the mix intent on dealing out their rough justice, but he saw Alec's problem. From what he'd seen of Jace and Alexander's showy sister, he was sure that Alec was used to protecting them, shielding them from their own rash actions, and that meant Alec was used to defending and not attacking.

"You'll do great without them," Magnus encouraged. "I can help you."

Alec looked skeptical about that, which was ridiculous since Magnus could do actual magic, something Shadowhunters liked to forget when they were deep in contemplation of how superior they were. To Alec's credit, though, he nodded and moved forward. Magnus noted, with slight puzzlement, that whenever Magnus tried to edge ahead, Alec put out an arm or moved slightly faster, staying in front of Magnus in a protective stance.

The people still in the bar were flattened against the walls as if pinned there, unmoving with terror. Someone was sobbing.

There was a low, rattling growl coming from the back lounge of the bar.

Alec crept toward the sound, Shadowhunter-soft and swift, and Magnus followed.

The lounge was decorated with black-and-white pictures of women from the 1950s and a disco ball that obviously provided no useful light. There was an empty stage made of boxes and a reading lamp that provided the only real illumination. There were couches in the center of the room, chairs at the back, and shadows all around.

There was a shadow moving and growling among all the other shadows. Alec prowled forward, hunting it, and the werewolf gave a growl of challenge.

And there was suddenly a slender girl with her hair in long dark coils, trailing ribbons and blood, dashing straight at them. Magnus leaped forward and caught her in his arms before she could distract or be attacked by Alec.

"Don't let him hurt her!" she screamed while at the same time Magnus asked, "How badly did she hurt you?"

Magnus paused and said, "We may be at somewhat of an impasse. Yes or no questions now: Are you badly hurt?"

He took hold of her shoulders gently and looked her over. She had a long, deep scratch all the way up one smooth brown arm. It was welling with blood, falling in fat drops to the floor as they spoke; she was the source of the blood on the floor outside.

She glared at him and lied, "No."

"You're a mundane, aren't you?"

"Yes—or I'm not a werewolf or anything else, if that's what you mean."

"But you know she's a werewolf."

"Yes, dumbass!" snapped the girl. "She told me. I know all about it. I don't care. It's my fault. I encouraged her to go out."

"I'm not the one encouraging werewolves to go out at the full moon and attack people on the dance floor," Magnus said. "But perhaps we can settle which of us is the dumbass at a better time when there are not lives at stake."

The girl clutched his arm. She could see Alec, visible as Shadowhunters almost never were to the mundanes. She could see his weapons. She was bleeding too much, and yet her fear was all for someone else.

Magnus held on to the girl's arm. He would have done better with ingredients and potions, but he sent blue crackling power twining around her arm to soothe the pain and stop the bleeding. When he opened his eyes he saw the girl's gaze fixed on him, her lips parted and her face wondering. Magnus wondered if she had even known that there were people who could do magic, that anything but werewolves existed in the world.

Over her shoulder he saw Alec lunge and join battle with the wolf.

"One last question," said Magnus, speaking rapidly and softly. "Can you trust me to see your friend safe?"

The girl hesitated, and then said, "Yes."

"Then go wait outside," said Magnus. "Outside the bar, not this room. Go wait outside and clear out everyone that you can. Tell people it's a stray dog that wandered in—give people the excuse they will all want to dismiss this. Tell them you're not badly hurt. What's your friend's name?"

She swallowed. "Marcy."

"Marcy will want to know you're safe, once we've got through to her," said Magnus. "Go for her sake."

The girl nodded, a sharp jerky movement, and then fled from Magnus's grip. He heard her platform heels hitting the tiles as she went. He was able, finally, to turn back to Alec.

He saw teeth flash in the dark and did not see Alec, because Alec was a blur of motion, rolling away, then coming back at the wolf.

At Marcy, Magnus thought, and at the same time he saw that Alec hadn't forgotten that Marcy was a person, or at least that Magnus had asked him to help her.

He wasn't using his seraph blades. He was trying not to hurt someone who had fangs and claws. Magnus did not want Alec to get scratched—and he definitely did not want to risk Alec getting bitten.

"Alexander," Magnus called, and realized his mistake when Alec turned his head and then had to back up hurriedly out of the way of the werewolf's vicious swipe at him. He tucked and rolled, landing in a crouch in front of Magnus.

"You have to stay back," he said, breathlessly.

The werewolf, taking advantage of Alec's distraction, growled and sprang. Magnus threw a ball of blue fire at her, knocking her back and sending her spinning. Some yells rose up from the few people still left in the bar, all of whom were hurrying toward the exits. Magnus didn't care. He knew Shadowhunters were meant to protect civilians, but Magnus was emphatically not one.

"You have to remember I'm a warlock."

"I know," Alec said, scanning the shadows. "I just want—" He wasn't making any sense, but the next sentence he spoke unfortunately made perfect sense. "I think," he said clearly, "I think you made her mad."

Magnus followed Alec's gaze. The werewolf was back on her feet and was stalking them, her eyes lit with unholy fire.

"Those are some excellent observational skills you have there, Alexander."

Alec tried to push Magnus back. Magnus caught hold of his black T-shirt and pulled Alec back with him. They moved together slowly out of the back lounge.

The werewolf's friend had been as good as her word: the bar was empty, a glittering shadowy playground for the werewolf to stalk them through.

Alec surprised Magnus and the werewolf both by

breaking away and lunging at Marcy. Whatever he had been planning, it didn't work: this time the werewolf's swipe caught him full in the chest. Alec went flying into a hot pink wall decorated with gold glitter. He hit a mirror set into the wall and decorated with curling gold fretwork with enough force to crack the glass across.

"Oh, stupid Shadowhunters," Magnus moaned under his breath. But Alec used his own body hitting the wall as leverage, rebounding off the wall and up, catching a sparkling chandelier and swinging, then dropping down as lightly as a leaping cat and crouching to attack again in one smooth movement. "Stupid, sexy Shadowhunters."

"Alec!" Magnus called. Alec had learned his lesson: he didn't look around or risk getting distracted. Magnus snapped his fingers, a dancing blue flame appearing from them as if he had snapped on a lighter. That caught Alec's attention. "Alexander. Let's do this together."

Magnus lifted his hands and cast a web of lucent blue lines from his fingers, to baffle the wolf and protect the mundanes. Each of the shimmering strings of light would give off enough of a magical charge to make the wolf hesitate.

Alec wove around them, and Magnus wove the light around him at the same time. He was surprised at the ease with which Alec moved with his magic. Almost every other Shadowhunter he had known had been a little wary and taken aback.

Maybe it was the fact that Magnus had never wished to help and protect in quite this way before, but the combination of Magnus's magic and Alec's strength worked, somehow.

The wolf snarled and ducked and whimpered, her world filled with blinding light, and everywhere she went, there Alec was. Magnus kind of knew how the wolf felt.

The wolf flagged and whimpered, a line of blue light cutting across her brindled fur, and Alec was on it. His knee pressed into the wolf's flank, and his hand went to his belt. Despite everything, fear flashed cold up Magnus's spine. He could picture the knife, and Alec cutting the werewolf's throat.

What Alec drew out was a rope. He wrapped it around the werewolf's neck as he held her pinned down with his body. She struggled and bucked and snarled. Magnus let the lines of magic drop and murmured, the magic words falling from his lips in fading puffs of blue smoke, spells of healing and soothing, illusions of safety and calm.

"Come on, Marcy," Magnus said clearly. "Come *on!*"

The werewolf shuddered and changed, bones popping and fur flowing away, and in a few long, agonizing moments Alec found himself with his arms wrapped around a girl dressed only in the torn ribbons of a dress.

She was very nearly naked.

Alec looked more uncomfortable than he had when she was a wolf. He let go quickly, and Marcy slid to a sitting position, her arms clutched around herself. She was whimpering under her breath. Magnus pulled off his long red leather coat and knelt to wrap it around her. Marcy clutched at the lapels.

"Thank you so much," said Marcy, looking up at Magnus with big beseeching eyes. She was a fetching little blonde in human form, which made her giant, angry wolf form seem funnier in retrospect. Then her face tightened with anguish, and nothing seemed funny at all. "Did I ... please, did I hurt anybody?"

"No," said Alec, his voice strong, confident as it only very rarely was. "No, you didn't hurt anyone at all."

"There was someone with me..." Marcy began.

"She was scratched," Magnus said, keeping his voice

steady and reassuring. "She's fine. I healed her."

"But I hurt her," Marcy said, and put her face in her blood-stained hands.

Alec reached out and touched Marcy's back, rubbing it gently as if this werewolf stranger was his own sister.

"She's fine," he said. "You didn't—I *know* you didn't want to hurt her, that you didn't want to hurt anyone. You can't help being what you are. You're going to figure it all out."

"She forgives you," Magnus told Marcy, but Marcy was looking at Alec.

"Oh my God, you're a Shadowhunter," she whispered, just as Erik the werewolf waiter had, but with fear in her voice instead of scorn. "What are you going to do to me?" She shut her eyes. "No. I'm sorry. You stopped me. If you hadn't been here—whatever you do to me, I deserve it."

"I'm not going to do anything to you," said Alec, and

Marcy opened her eyes and looked up into Alec's face. "I meant what I said. I'm not going to tell anyone. I promise."

Alec had looked the same when Magnus had spoken of his childhood at the party when they had first met. It was something Magnus hardly ever did, but he had felt spiky and defensive about the advent of all these Shadowhunters in his house, at Jocelyn Fray's daughter, Clary, showing up without her mother and with so many questions she deserved answers to. He had not expected to look into a Shadowhunter's eyes and see sympathy.

Marcy sat up, gathering the coat around her. She looked suddenly dignified, as if she had realized she had rights in this situation. That she was a person. That she was a soul, and that soul had been respected as it should have been.

"Thank you," she said calmly. "Thank you both."

"Marcy?" said her friend's voice from the door.

Marcy looked up. "Adrienne!"

Adrienne dashed inside, almost skidding on the tiled floor, and threw herself to the ground and enveloped Marcy in her arms.

"Are you hurt? Show me," Marcy whispered into her shoulder.

"It's fine, it's nothing, it's absolutely all right," said Adrienne, stroking Marcy's hair.

"I'm so sorry," said Marcy, cupping Adrienne's face. They kissed, heedless of the fact that Alec and Magnus were standing right there.

When they broke apart, Adrienne rocked Marcy in her arms and whispered, "We'll figure this out so it never happens again. We will."

Other people followed Adrienne's lead and came in by twos and threes.

"You're pretty snappily dressed for a dogcatcher," said a man Magnus thought was the bartender.

Magnus inclined his head. "Thank you very much."

More people swirled back in, cautiously at first and then in far greater numbers. Nobody was asking where exactly the dog had gone. A great many of them seemed to want drinks.

Perhaps some of them would ask questions later, when the shock had worn off, and this night's work would become a situation that needed clearing up. But Magnus decided that was a problem for later.

"That was nice, what you said to her," said Magnus, when the crowd had completely hidden Marcy and Adrienne from their sight.

"Uh ... it was nothing," said Alec, shifting and looking embarrassed. The Shadowhunters did not see much to approve of in kindness, Magnus supposed. "I mean, that's what we're here for, aren't we? Shadowhunters, I mean. We have to help anyone who needs help. We have to protect people."

The Nephilim Magnus had known had seemed to believe the Downworlders were created to help *them*, and to be disposed of if they didn't help enough.

Magnus looked at Alec. He was sweaty and still breathing a little hard, the scratches on his arms and face healing quickly thanks to the *iratzes* on his skin.

"I don't think we're going to get a drink in here; there's much too long a line," said Magnus slowly. "Let's have a nightcap back at my place."

They walked home. Though it was a long way, it was a nice walk on a summer night, the air warm on Magnus's bare arms and the moon turning the Brooklyn Bridge into a highway of shining white.

"I'm really glad your friend called you to help that

girl," Alec confessed as they walked. "I'm really glad you asked me along. I was—I was surprised you did, after how things were going before."

"I was worried you were having a terrible time," Magnus told him. It felt like putting a lot of power in Alec's hands, but Alec was honest with him and Magnus found himself possessed by the strange impulse to be honest back.

"No," said Alec, and went red. "No, that's not it at all. Did I seem— I'm sorry."

"Don't be sorry," Magnus told him softly.

Words seemed to explode out of Alec in a rush, though judging by his expression he wished he could hold them back. "It was my fault. I got everything wrong even before I showed up, and you knew how to order at the restaurant and I had to stop myself laughing at that song on the subway. I have no idea what I'm doing and you're, um, glamorous."

"What?"

Alec looked at Magnus, stricken, as if he thought he'd got everything wrong again.

Magnus wanted to say, *No, I was the one who brought you to a terrible restaurant and treated you like a mundane because I didn't know how to date a Shadowhunter and almost bailed on you even though you were brave enough to ask me out in the first place.*

What Magnus actually ended up saying was, "I thought that terrible song was *hilarious*," and he threw back his head and laughed. He glanced over at Alec and found him laughing too. His whole face changed when he laughed, Magnus thought. Nobody had to be sorry for anything, not tonight.

When they reached Magnus's home, Magnus laid a hand on the front door and it swung open.

"I lost my keys maybe fifteen years ago," Magnus explained.

He really should get around to getting more keys cut. He didn't really need them, though, and it had been a long time since there was anyone he wanted to have his keys—to have ready access to his home because he wanted them there anytime they wanted to come. There had been nobody since Etta, half a century ago.

Magnus gave Alec a sidelong look as they climbed the rickety stairs. Alec caught the glance, and his breathing quickened; his blue eyes were bright. Alec bit his lower lip, and Magnus stopped walking.

It was only a momentary hesitation. But then Alec reached out and caught his arm, fingers tight above his elbow.

"Magnus," he said in a low voice.

Magnus realized that Alec was mirroring the way

Magnus had taken hold of Alec's arms on Tuesday: on the day of Alec's first kiss.

Magnus's breath caught in his throat.

That was apparently all the encouragement Alec needed. He leaned in, expression open and ardent in the darkness of the stairs, in the hush of this moment. Alec's mouth met Magnus's, soft and gentle. Getting his breath back was an impossibility, and no longer a priority.

Magnus closed his eyes and unbidden images came to him: Alec trying not to laugh on the subway, Alec's startled appreciation at the taste of new food, Alec glad not to be ditched, Alec sitting on the floor with and telling a werewolf that she could not help what she was. Magnus found himself almost afraid at the thought of what he had nearly done in almost leaving Alec before the evening was over. Leaving Alec was the last thing he wanted to do right now. He pulled in Alec by the belt loops of his jeans, closed all distance between their bodies and caught Alec's tiny needful gasp with his mouth.

The kiss caught fire and all he could see behind his closed eyes were gold sparks; all he was aware of was Alec's mouth, Alec's strong gentle hands that had held down a werewolf and tried not to hurt her, Alec pressing him against the banister so the rotten wood creaked alarmingly and Magnus did not even care—Alec here, Alec now, the taste of Alec in his mouth, his hands pushing aside the fabric of his own worn T-shirt to get at Alec's bare skin underneath.

It took an embarrassingly long time before they both remembered that Magnus had an apartment, and tumbled toward it without disentangling from each other. Magnus blew the door open without looking at it: the door banged so hard against the wall that Magnus cracked an eye open to check that he had not absentmindedly made his front door explode.

Alec kissed a sweet careful line down Magnus's neck, starting from just below his ear to the hollow at the base of his throat. The door was fine. Everything was great.

Magnus pulled Alec down to the sofa, Alec collapsing bonelessly on top of him. Magnus fastened his lips to Alec's neck. He tasted of sweat and soap and skin, and Magnus bit down, hoping to leave a mark on the pale skin there, wanting to. Alec gave a breathy whimper and pushed his body into the contact. Magnus's hands slid up under Alec's rumpled shirt, learning the shape of Alec's body. He ran his fingers over the swell of Alec's shoulders and down the long lean curve of his back, feeling the scars of his profession and the wildness of his kisses. Shyly, Alec undid the buttons on Magnus's waistcoat, laying skin bare and slipping inside to touch Magnus's chest, his stomach, and Magnus felt cool silk replaced by warm hands, curious and caressing. He felt Alec's fingers shaking against his skin.

Magnus reached up and pressed his hand against Alec's cheek, his brown bejeweled fingers a contrast to Alec's moonlight-pale skin: Alec turned his face into the curve of Magnus's palm and kissed it, and Magnus's heart broke.

"Alexander," he murmured, wanting to say more than just "Alec," to call him by a name that was longer than and different from the name everybody else called him, a name with weight and value to it. He whispered the name as if making a promise that he would take his time. "Maybe we should wait a second."

He pushed Alec, just slightly, but Alec took the hint. He took it much further than Magnus had meant it. He scrambled off the sofa and away from Magnus.

"Did I do something wrong?" Alec asked, and his voice was shaking too.

"No," Magnus said. "Far from it."

"Are you sending me home?"

Magnus held up his hands. "I have no interest in telling you what to do, Alexander. I don't want to persuade you to do anything or convince you not to do anything. I'm just saying that you might want to stop and think for a moment. And then you can decide—whatever you want to decide."

Alec looked frustrated. Magnus could sympathize.

Then he scrubbed both hands through his hair—it was already a wreck thanks to Magnus; there was no ruining it any further; it had reached maximum ruination—and paced the floor. He was thinking, Magnus saw, and tried not to wonder what he was thinking of: Jace, Magnus, his family or his duty, how to be kind to himself.

He stopped pacing when he reached Magnus's doorway.

"I should probably go home," said Alec eventually.

"Probably," said Magnus, with great regret.

"I don't want to," Alec said.

"I don't want you to," said Magnus. "But if you don't..."

Alec nodded, quickly. "Good-bye, then," he said, and leaned down for a quick kiss. At least Magnus suspected it was supposed to be quick. He wasn't entirely sure what happened after that, but somehow he was wrapped around Alec entirely and they were on the floor. Alec was gasping and clutching at him, and somebody's hands were on someone else's belt buckle and Alec kissed Magnus so hard he tasted blood, and Magnus said, "Oh, *God*," and then—

And then Alec was back up on his feet and had hold of the doorframe, as if the air had become a tide that might rush him back to Magnus if he didn't grab at some support. He seemed to be struggling with something, and Magnus wondered whether he was going to ask to stay after all or say the whole night had been a mistake. Magnus felt more fear and more anticipation than he was entirely able to play off, and he realized it mattered more than it should, so soon.

He waited, tense, and Alec said, "Can I see you again?"

The words tumbled out in a rush, shy and eager and entirely uncertain of what Magnus would answer, and Magnus felt the headlong rush of adrenaline and excitement that came from the start of a new adventure.

"Yes," said Magnus, still lying on the floor. "I'd like that."

"Um," said Alec, "so—next Friday night?"

"Well..."

Alec looked instantly worried, as if he thought Magnus was going to take it all back and say that actually he had changed his mind. He was beautiful and hopeful and hesitant, a heartbreaker who wore his heart on his sleeve. Magnus found himself wanting to show his hand, to take a risk and be vulnerable. He recognized and accepted this strange new feeling: that he would rather be hurt himself than hurt Alec.

"Friday night would be fine," Magnus said, and Alec smiled his brilliant, light-up-the-world smile and backed out of the apartment, still looking at Magnus. He backed up all the way to the top of the stairs. There was a yell, but Magnus had already risen and closed the door before he could see Alec fall down the steps, as that was the sort of thing a man had to do in private.

He did lean on the windowsill, though, and watch Alec emerge from his building's front door, tall and pale and messy-haired, and walk off down Greenpoint Avenue, whistling off-key. And Magnus found himself hoping.

He had been taught so many times that hope was foolish, but he could not help it, as heedless as a child straying close to the fire and stubbornly refusing to learn from experience. Maybe this time was different—maybe this love was different. It felt so different; surely that had to mean something. Maybe the year to come would be a good year for both of them. Maybe this time things would work out the way Magnus wanted them to.

Maybe Alexander Lightwood would not break his heart.

Discover the world of
the Shadowhunters...

A MAGNUS BANE STORY

The
**Midnight
Heir**

CASSANDRA CLARE
SARAH REES BRENNAN

Magnus had vowed never
to return to London...
Now he remembers why.

A dark tale from Cassandra Clare's

Shadowhunter world.

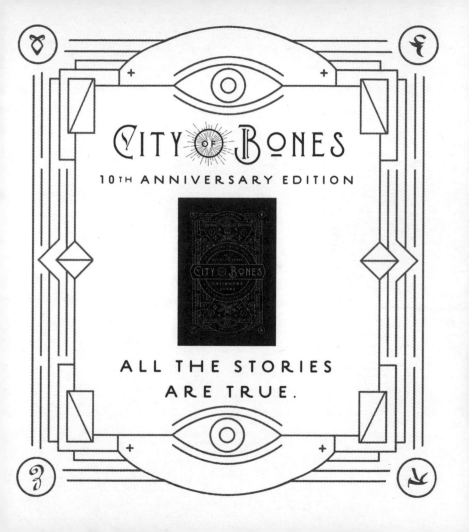